WANTED:
Valeeta, rebel spy.

CRIME:
Treason.

WHEREABOUTS:
The Glorid city on
planet Delbor.

YOUR MISSION:
Capture Valeeta before
she can take over the planet.

Bantam Books in the
Be An Interplanetary Spy Series

REBEL SPY

by Len Neufeld
illustrated by Alex Nino

A Byron Preiss Book

BANTAM BOOKS
TORONTO · NEW YORK · LONDON · SYDNEY

To ECL, JMRN and JPLN

Len Neufeld is a free-lance writer and editor living in Brooklyn, New York with his wife Elynn, and two sons, Joshua and Jacob, who keep his head on the ground and his feet in the clouds. He is best known as an ex-poet and the indexer of the Great Soviet Encyclopedia.

Alex Nino, a native of the Philippines, has long delighted fantasy readers with his surrealistic and realistic illustrations in graphic story form for Heavy Metal, DC, Marvel Comics, and in the new *Time Machine* series for Bantam Books.

RL 3, IL age 9 and up

REBEL SPY

A Bantam Book/June 1984

Special thanks to Ron Buehl, Lisa Novak, Anne Greenberg, Lucy Salvino, Ann Weil and Pauline Bigornia.

Cover art by Steve Fastner

Cover design by Alex Jay

Logo and series design by Marc Hempel

Book mechanical production and additional design by Susan Hui Leung

Typesetting by David E. Seham Associates, Inc.

"Be An Interplanetary Spy" is a trademark of Byron Preiss Visual Publications, Inc.

ISBN 0-553-24198-2

Published simultaneously in the United States and Canada

PRINTED IN THE UNITED STATES OF AMERICA

0 9 8 7 6 5 4 3 2 1

Introduction

You are an Interplanetary Spy. You are about to embark on a dangerous mission. On your mission you will face challenges that may result in your death.

You work for the Interplanetary Spy Center , a far-reaching organization devoted to stopping crime and terrorism in the galaxy. While you are on your mission, you will take your orders from the Interplanetary Spy Center. Follow your instructions carefully.

You will be traveling alone on your mission. If you are captured, the Interplanetary Spy Center will not be able to help you. Only your wits and your sharp spy skills will help you reach your goal. Be careful. Keep your eyes open at all times.

If you are ready to meet the challenge of being an Interplanetary Spy, turn to Page 1.

TOP
SECRET

You are traveling through sector 14 with
Callisto, a level 5 Interplanetary Spy. You
are returning in a two-passenger starship
from an awards ceremony on the planet
Mirado, on your way to Spy Center.
To begin your mission, enter your
Interplanetary Spy ISBN number below.
If you are not sure of your number,
check the back cover of this book.

Turn to page 2.

Callisto is checking your ship's computer signals. "Look at the alert panel," he says.

You see the ultrasecret alert glowing. You throw a switch. A voice comes from a speaker on the computer console.

"Attention all Spies in sector 14. The dangerous ex-Interplanetary Spy Valeeta has been tracked to the planet Delbor, in the Aramon system. This rebel Spy has threatened to destroy the Interplanetary Spy organization. Your mission is to capture Valeeta.

Valeeta

Go on to the next page.

"An Interplanetary Spy agent already on Delbor will give you the information you need for your mission. Send your ship's code name to the agent on Delbor, and he will tell you where to land your ship."

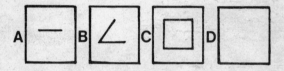

To get your ship's code name, press the shape that will complete the sequence on the screen.

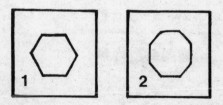

Do you press shape 1? Turn to page 18.

Do you press shape 2? Turn to page 39.

4 You drive northwest. Soon you and the king are lost in the desert . . . until a gorm finds you!

The End

You have made a bad mistake, Spy! The agent on Delbor cannot believe that you're a real Spy. The landing coordinates he sends you set you down in a very warm place—a volcano!

Your disguise will dissolve at high skin temperatures. You have been trained by Spy Center to raise your skin temperature by self-hypnosis.

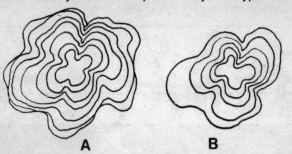

A   **B**

You must imagine the temperature pattern that is hotter than 120 kad-degrees. But be careful! If you imagine the wrong pattern, your disguise will stay on forever!

(Each line represents 20 kad-degrees.)

Do you imagine pattern A?
Turn to page 69.

Do you imagine pattern B?
Turn to page 36.

You climb through and emerge on the desert.

The Glorid city is an immense domed fortress. You walk around the walls until you see an entrance with receptacles for the keys.

Turn to page 19.

You have set off the power car's antitampering device. A stun gas shoots out at you! You fall asleep. By the time you wake up, this mission will be over.

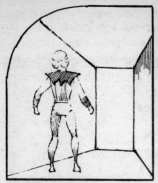

Dead end, Spy!

A barrier drops down behind you.

There's nothing for you to do here.

You grow bored.

Very bored.

Your multikon registers a beeping signal coming from the center of the city. You hire a Choonian Nuba-cab and follow the signal.

Turn to page 13.

The king returns with you to your power car. You must drive back to the landing area to meet Callisto.

Do you drive northwest?
Turn to page 4.

Do you drive southwest?
Turn to page 35.

(If you can't remember, check the map on page 20.)

You press four shapes, but the gate remains locked.

You try to squeeze through the bars of the gate. Unfortunately, the head part of your disguise is scraped off.

The End

A group of Choons doesn't like your looks!

The signal seems to be coming from a large palace. You tell the driver to stop there.

You take some money from your wallet and reach forward to pay the driver, but he grabs your arm! He waves to two guards in front of the palace.

The guards approach and talk with the driver. They take hold of you, and one of them says, "We've got this intruder." They bring you into the palace.

Turn to page 15.

The End

Inside the palace, the guards search you and take your multikon. Then they bring you to the king of the Choons.

"Who are you?" says the king. "Why have you come here? And what is this device?"

You tell the king that the Choons and all of Delbor are in terrible danger. Valeeta, an interplanetary criminal, has entered the Glorid city.

"Where have you heard such things?" asks the king. "You are just an ordinary Choon."

You must remove your disguise to show the king you are not a Choon.

Turn to page 6.

The Poddians' ship glides swiftly along the river. One of the Poddians points to four holes on the roof of the cavern. The Poddians' thoughts sound in your mind: "The hole that is unlike the others leads to the surface of the desert close to the Glorid city. The others lead to death!"

Do you climb through here? Turn to page 37.

Do you climb through here? Turn to page 7.

You set your course—it's the last mistake you'll ever make! You've landed in a quicksand bog in the Great North Swamp.

It's slow . . . but final!

The End

"What's the matter with you?" Callisto says angrily. "As a level 2 Spy you should be able to perform these simple functions. Now I have to reset the computer. Next time, do it right!"

Turn to page 39.

You must insert the keys in the proper receptacles. The lines on the keys must cross all of the points in the receptacles.

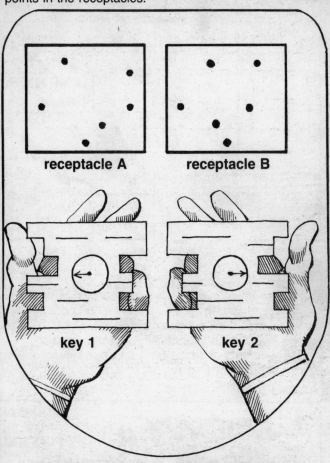

receptacle A   receptacle B

key 1   key 2

**Do you insert key 1 in receptacle A
and key 2 in receptacle B?**
Turn to page 38.

**Do you insert key 1 in receptacle B
and key 2 in receptacle A?**
Turn to page 92.

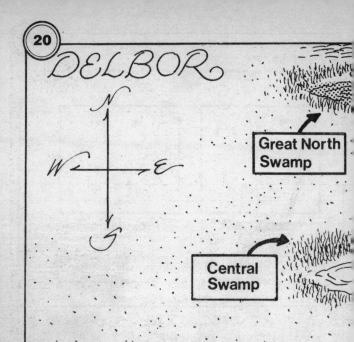

DELBOR

Great North Swamp

Central Swamp

You type in the code name correctly and send the signal. The agent on Delbor sends back a map of the planet, which appears on your computer screen. At the bottom of the map is an enlarged view of the area where you are to land.

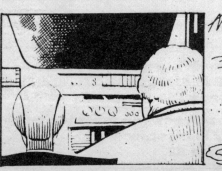

MOUNTAIN
AND
FOOTHILLS

SANDY
DESERT
DUNES

STONY
DESERT

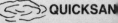

QUICKSAN

Do you land in the north?
Turn to page 17.

Do you land near the center?
Turn to page 25.

⊙	**ACTIVE VOLCANO**
⬡	**GLORIDS' CITY**
©	**CHOONS**
®	**RO-ZINS**

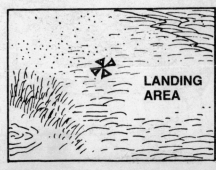

LANDING AREA

You cautiously walk into the city. A shadow crosses your path, and you look up. A giant torloo is swooping down on you!

You run toward a nearby building and fall flat.

The torloo crashes into the side of the building!

Go on to the next page.

When you get up, you notice a flickering light coming from inside the building. You go in.

On a screen in a large auditorium, you see pictures of the time when the Glorids lived in the city.

A large building appears on the screen. Inside that building, Glorid scientists work on their machines.

Turn to page 24.

24 Valeeta is trying to master Glorid science. Perhaps she is in that building.

A view of the entire city appears on the screen. Before the picture changes, you must locate the building.

Is the building in this direction? Turn to page 40.

Is the building in this direction? Turn to page 61.

You bring your ship to a landing near the Central Swamp.

The agent is waiting for you. He shows you his Interplanetary Spy badge and says, "You may call me Qubex."

Callisto examines the badge and gives his approval.

Turn to page 26.

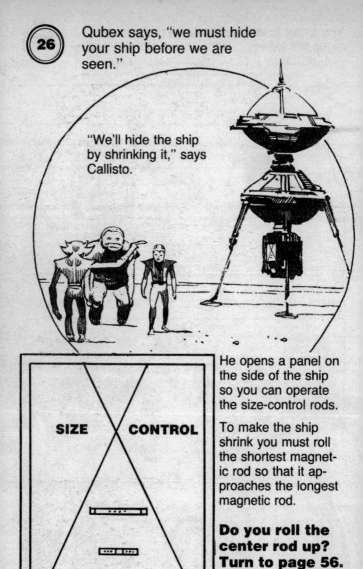

Qubex says, "we must hide your ship before we are seen."

"We'll hide the ship by shrinking it," says Callisto.

He opens a panel on the side of the ship so you can operate the size-control rods.

To make the ship shrink you must roll the shortest magnetic rod so that it approaches the longest magnetic rod.

SIZE CONTROL

MAGNETIC RODS

Do you roll the center rod up? Turn to page 56.

Do you roll the center rod down? Turn to page 31.

You come to the mountains and ride north along the foothills. Between two hills you spot a dark entrance in the shadows of tall plants.

You stop your car and hide it among some trees. You approach the entrance. You peer into the blackness, but you can see nothing.

You walk toward the darkness.

Turn to page 28.

As you enter, you discover that the blackness is just a dark area at the entrance. Inside is a brightly lit space.

Suddenly you hear a voice in your head: "Prepare for the mind maze!"

Another doorway appears in the opposite wall. A glowing image of a maze seems to hang in the air over it.

Turn to page 48.

You make a bridge and start across, but you can't reach the other side.

You try to go back, but you lose your balance and fall into the river. The current carries you away! Goodbye, Spy!

The End

You'll never get to Delbor this way, Spy! Other Spies are arriving there now. It's no longer your mission.

The ship shrinks to a tiny size, and Callisto hides it in the sand.

Callisto sets his multikon so he can use it to find the ship at any time. You set yours, too.

Qubex says, "Follow me. I have power cars and disguises for you. But first, I will tell you about your mission."

Turn to page 32.

Qubex flips open a miniscreen. He says, "Two races live on Delbor—the Choons and the Ro-zins. They have always been enemies. Some time ago, Delbor was visited by now-vanished aliens called the Glorids. The Glorids wanted to end the fighting between the Choons and the Ro-zins. So the Glorids closed off the mountain passes with mazes.

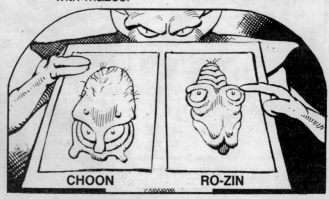

CHOON   **RO-ZIN**

"The Glorids built a city near the Great North Swamp. The city is deserted now except for some wild animals, but it keeps itself going with automatic machinery.

Go on to the next page.

"The Glorids told the two races that when they become wise enough to make peace, they will be able to go through the mazes, enter the city, and learn about the wonders of Glorid science inside. The Glorids gave the kings of the two races each a key. The two keys must be used together to enter the city."

Turn to page 34.

Spy

Callisto

Qubex picks up a spray-on disguise machine and sets the controls. He sprays a Ro-zin disguise on Callisto and a Choon disguise on you.

"When Valeeta came to Delbor," continues Qubex, "she found a way to dig into the Glorid city. You must go to the city of the Choons, and Callisto must go to the city of the Ro-zins. You must each get a key so that together you can enter the city and capture Valeeta. She is learning the secrets of Glorid science. You must stop her before she becomes too powerful."

Turn to page 59.

You drive southwest. Soon you are approaching the landing area.

As you come over the top of a dune, you can see the Ro-zins trying to capture Callisto. You see that he's already taken off his Ro-zin disguise. Callisto has the Glorid key!

Turn to page 80.

You imagine pattern B, but its five lines add up to only 100 kad-degrees.

You are trapped forever.

You tumble over the edge of the hole. You are falling into Delbor's molten core!

It's a long way down. You have plenty of time to think about your error!

The End

You insert the key, and the entrance opens. But so does the floor!

A large, hungry gratz is so glad you dropped in!

The End

Callisto sees that you have pressed shape 2. He says, "That's right, Spy. Each figure has twice as many sides as the one before it."

The screen goes blank for a moment. Then the ship's code name appears.

SEARCHER

You ask Callisto if he has ever seen Valeeta. He says, "No. But as a level 5 Spy I was told about her rebellion. Nobody knows why she has turned against us."

Now you must plot the ship's course. Delbor is in area C4 of sector 14. Your ship is in area A2. You must plot a straight course from your ship's position to Delbor.

	1	2	3	4
A		●←			Ship
B				
C				●Delbor
D				

Do you pass through area B2? Turn to page 41.

Do you pass through area A3? Turn to page 30.

You head in the wrong direction.

City dragons love lost Spies!

The End

"Well done, Spy," says Callisto. "You are a skillful pilot. Our Spy skills must be sharp for this mission. We have no weapons on board, but I was given these experimental multikons on Mirado. They can send and receive signals at all wavelengths. We can use them to communicate on Delbor. Take this one."

Turn to page 42.

42

Now you are approaching Delbor. Get ready to signal the agent on the planet.

Go on to the next page.

Callisto tells you to send the signal while he prepares the ship for landing.

You must type the ship's code name into the computer. How many more lines must you type onto the ship's computer screen in order to complete the code name? If you're not sure, check page 39.

19? Turn to page 20.

(44)

"I explored the Poddian tunnels until I found one that passes under the city's walls. Then I dug into the city. Inside, I learned how the Glorids controlled energies one million times as powerful as the energies the Spies can control.

"All Glorid high-energy devices are operated with keys. I was able to turn many of the Glorid devices into weapons, but I needed the keys to use them. And I wasn't able to make more keys—the greatest products of Glorid science!

"I sent my false message to the Spies, so they would get the keys for me. I didn't want to risk my own life." She sneers at you. "You are the only Spy who has made it this far!"

Valeeta calls Qubex over and then says to you, "I am going to show you a generator the Glorids built to help turn Delbor into a garden planet. It was supposed to release its energy slowly over thousands of kad-years.

Go on to the next page.

"With these keys, I will set the generator to release all its energy in one giant explosion. Delbor and everything on it will be no more, while I escape with the secrets of Glorid science!

"Safe in space I will watch your final moments. Then at my hidden laboratory I will build more high-energy weapons. Soon I will defeat the Spies. No one else can oppose me. I will control the galaxy!"

She says to you, "Qubex is a Glorid android. I changed his circuits to make him serve me."

She orders Qubex, "Take the Spy to the generator chamber."

Qubex drags you out of the room.

Turn to page 52.

The vine was too long!

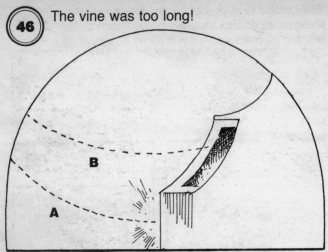

The noise of your fall alerts Valeeta's pet—a wild ogar!

You rotate the keys, but the six hours are up!
The generator clicks loudly . . . and then is
silent. You have succeeded!

Valeeta's sight returns in time to witness your triumph.
"Spy Center must have known about my plans after
all!" she exclaims in disbelief. "There's no other way
you could have defeated me!"

You and Callisto ignore Valeeta's
words and put her in the power car.
You rejoin the Ro-zins and the king
of the Choons at the city entrance.

Turn to page 88.

You study the maze for a long time. You think you have memorized the correct path, when the image disappears.

Left

Right

Do you begin by going left?
Turn to page 9.

Right? Turn to page 71.

Straight ahead? Turn to page 14.

Suddenly lights flash on! A net falls over you!

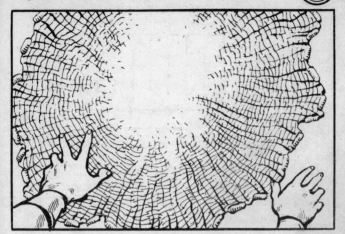

You are lifted into the air!

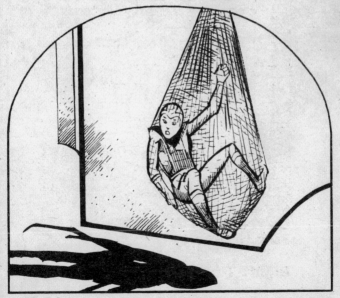

Turn to page 85.

Your power car starts up. You speed across the Delborean desert!

The sound of the power car awakens a sand-dragon, but it's too slow to catch you.

Turn to page 27.

To disarm the generator you must insert the keys so that the arrows on the keys point to the zeros in the receptacles.

Then you must rotate the keys the longest possible distance to make its arrow point to the x's in the receptacles.

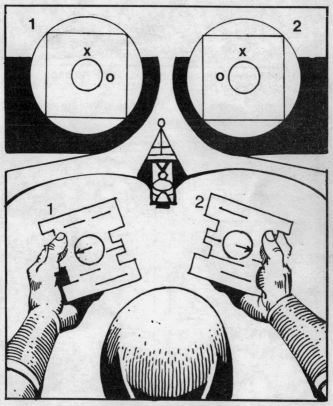

Do you rotate key 1 clockwise and key 2 counterclockwise?
Turn to page 87.

Do you rotate key 2 clockwise and key 1 counterclockwise?
Turn to page 47.

The Glorid generator is a huge machine resting in a pit in the floor of the chamber.

Qubex attaches the edge of the net to the surface of the generator. You can't get out!

Valeeta places the keys in receptacles on the generator. She rotates the keys carefully and then removes them and puts them in her pocket.

She looks at you and says, "You have six kad-hours. Enjoy them!"

Turn to page 64.

You turned the wrong bar!
The door shoots powerful bolts of energy at you.

Very powerful!

The End

You are going too fast! Your skimcraft flips over!

You are thrown clear, but the skimcraft is wrecked.

You get up and run to Callisto.

Turn to page 115.

Careless Spy! You didn't notice that only one arrow moves each time. The locator panel goes blank. You have no way of finding Valeeta!

Callisto would know what to do. Perhaps you can rescue him from the Ro-zins. You head for your landing area, where you last saw him.

Turn to page 102.

Nothing happens . . .
until a sand-dragon shows up!

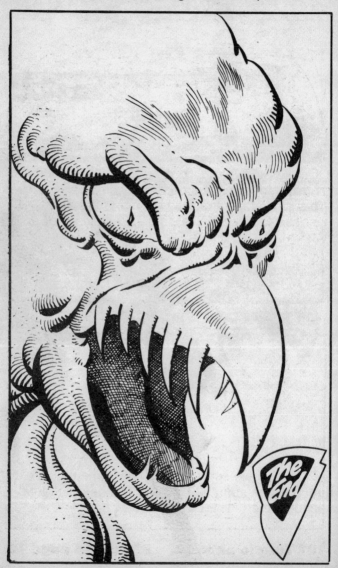

The End

You pressed the correct shapes, and the lock snaps open. Now you must find the key.

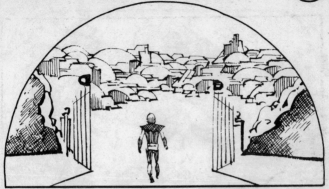

The key was made by Glorid scientists. Perhaps it gives off special rays. Your multikon can scan all wavelengths and detect any rays that may be given off by the key.

To set your multikon you must press the button showing the number of square corners in the shape on the screen.

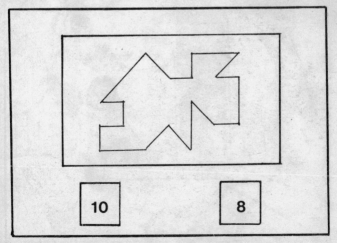

10

8

10? Turn to page 10.   8? Turn to page 72.

Valeeta's ogar leaps to stop you. You throw the net over it and escape!

You must find Valeeta, get the keys back, and disarm the generator.

Turn to page 65.

Qubex shows you how to operate the power cars. He gives each of you a wallet and says: "With this money and the information I've given you, you should be able to get the keys and complete your mission. I must return to my station and meet any other Spies who land. Good luck!" Qubex drives away.

You and Callisto agree to meet here at the landing area after you have gotten the keys. You climb into the power cars.

Turn to page 60.

To start your power car you must fit the starter tab into the correct tab-lock.

Tab-lock A? Turn to page 50.

Tab-lock B? Turn to page 8.

You see the Glorid science building on the
screen. You go up to the roof of the building
you are in and look across the city. It's a long
way to the science building.

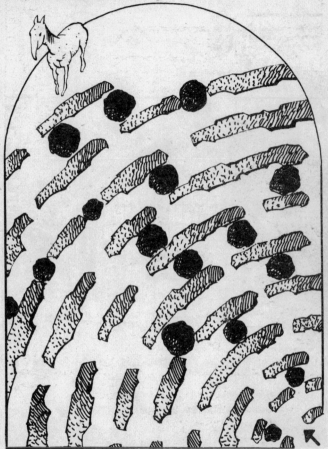

You see a wild joujan on the other side of a fenced-in
field of pits and high walls. If you can reach the joujan,
you might be able to ride it to your destination.

Is there a path to the joujan?
Yes? Turn to page 100.
No? Turn to page 119.

You step through the doorway and climb a stairway. You see a large, locked gate, crowned with the symbol of the Choons.

You must wait till night falls, so you can approach the gate without being seen.

Go on to the next page.

When darkness comes, you go up to the gate and examine the lock.

To open it, you must press the four shapes that will fit together to form the symbol of the Choons.

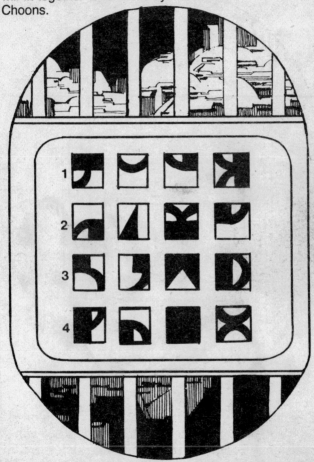

Do you find the shapes in rows 1, 3, and 4?
Turn to page 12.

Do you find the shapes in rows 1, 2, and 4?
Turn to page 57.

Valeeta and Qubex leave. The ogar remains, to make sure you don't escape.

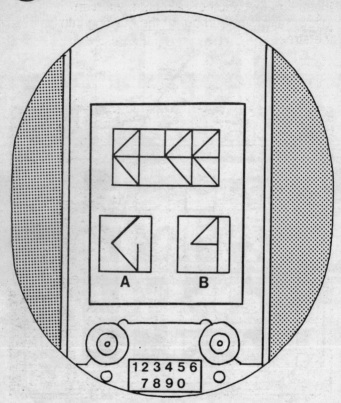

Quickly you use your multikon to analyze the force that holds the edge of the net to the generator. You can cancel the force by sending the correct signal. Press the shape that will complete the pattern on the screen.

Press shape A? Turn to page 58.

Press shape B? Turn to page 103.

From a window you see Valeeta and Qubex speeding away in a Glorid skimcraft. If you can find another skimcraft, you can follow them. You run out of the building into the street.

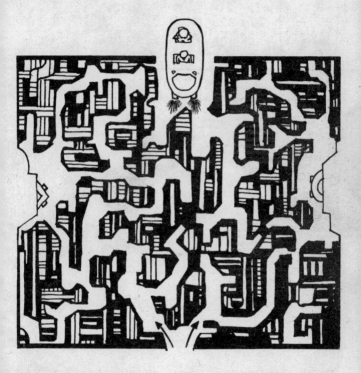

Do you go this way to find another skimcraft? Turn to page 40.

Do you go this way? Turn to page 97.

You crush a leaf in your fingers and let the juice drip into Callisto's mouth. Slowly he revives. He says, "Thanks, Spy. Without you, I would have been finished off by the desert heat."

You tell Callisto that Valeeta has set the Glorid generator to blow up Delbor. Now there are only four kad-hours left!

You and Callisto quickly tend to the injured Ro-zins and the king of the Choons. Callisto asks you how you got to the Glorid city. You tell him about the Poddians and your meeting with Valeeta and Qubex.

Turn to page 78.

You activate the correct squares.
Valeeta and Qubex are far ahead of you now.
You race after them.

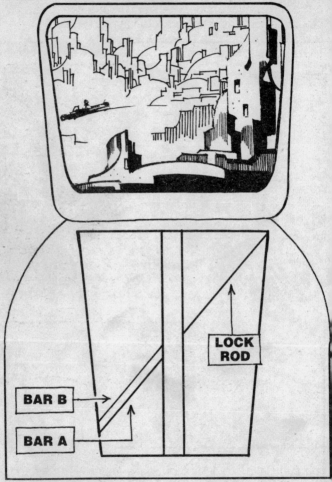

LOCK ROD

BAR B

BAR A

You come to an exit port in the wall of the city. You can open the port by turning the bar that is in line with the lock-rod.

Bar A? Turn to page 109.
Bar B? Turn to page 53.

You imagine the pattern made up of seven lines (140 kad-degrees). Your disguise turns into powder. The king is very surprised. "You are clearly not a Choon," he says. "You approached my palace openly and have honestly revealed yourself to me. I will trust you." He gives you back your multikon.

You tell the king that you and your partner, Callisto, are Interplanetary Spies, fighting crime and maintaining peace throughout the galaxy. You tell him that you are seeking the Glorid keys so you can enter the Glorid city and capture Valeeta.

The king says, "The key is useless to my people because the maze stops us from reaching the Ro-zins." He stands up and says, "Please come with me."

Turn to page 70.

The king takes you into the depths of the palace. He says, "This criminal Valeeta must be stopped.

"I will give you the key on one condition—that you take me with you through the maze. I want to meet with the Ro-zins. It is time to make peace!"

Turn to page 11.

Good work, Spy! You memorized the maze correctly, and you quickly walk through.

Once again, you come to a black doorway.

Turn to page 62.

You press the button showing the number 8. Your multikon doesn't register any signal. You decide to try once more before you give up.

Go back to page 57 and try again.

You can cross the river by using two pieces of driftwood to make a bridge. You must lay the driftwood across the tops of the stones that rise above the surface of the water.

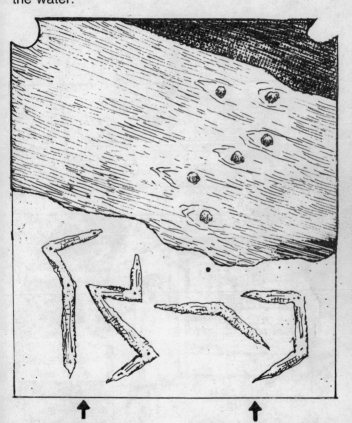

Do you use these pieces A and B? Turn to page 84.

Do you use these pieces C and D? Turn to page 29.

You swing through the window into a dimly lit room.

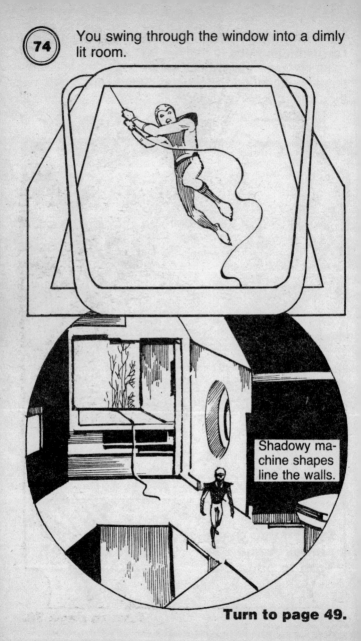

Shadowy machine shapes line the walls.

Turn to page 49.

Turn to page 76.

You hear a voice in your mind: "I am the queen of the Poddians. We live in the caverns of Delbor. We know about Valeeta because she entered the Glorid city by digging up into it from one of our tunnels. I can see in your thoughts that you are Valeeta's enemy. We will help you."

Go on to the next page.

The queen leads you to a boat on the river and tells you to get on board. "My sailors will take you near the Glorid city," she says. "You must go into the city alone, since we die if we leave the light of our caves."

Turn to page 16.

Callisto says, "I will go to the Glorid city. Perhaps—even if you fail—I will be able to enter the city and disarm the generator."

You describe the Glorid science building to Callisto, so he can find the generator.

Callisto points east. He says, "Take one of the power cars. I saw Valeeta and Qubex go in that direction before I lost consciousness."

Turn to page 94.

The Poddians have set fire to Valeeta's spaceship!

Valeeta and Qubex are after them! You get out of your power car and run to help the Poddians.

Turn to page 117.

80 You stop your power car and run to help Callisto. He shouts, "It's too late. Take the key. You must go on with the mission yourself!"

He throws the key to you. It sails over your head.

Go on to the next page.

You run and pick up the key. Some of the Ro-zins chase you. Others run up the dune and grab the king of the Choons. The king and Callisto have both been captured!

You see a dark opening in the ground. Maybe it's a sand-dragon's den, but you have nowhere else to hide.

Turn to page 82.

You jump into the opening and roll down a steep slope.

You're in an underground cavern. The rock walls give off a strange light.

Across the river, you can see passage-ways that might take you near the Glorid city. But the current is too strong for swimming.

Turn to page 73.

Good work, Spy! You dash eastward. Finally you see the foothills in the distance. Only three kad-hours remain!

Through a gap in the hills you see smoke and flames.

Turn to page 79.

Well done, Spy! You cross the river.

You set off through one of the underground passages.

Turn to page 75.

You hear a sound behind you. You twist around in the net. It is Valeeta!

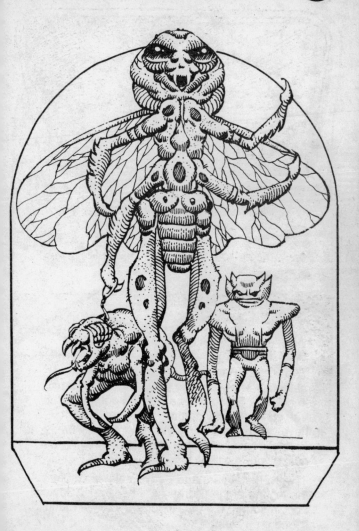

Turn to page 86.

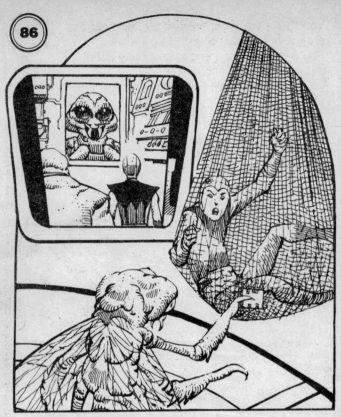

"You have fallen into my trap, Spy!" says Valeeta. "The message you received telling you to come to Delbor was a fake! I sent it." As Valeeta approaches you she says, "I see you have brought me the keys." She takes them from your pocket. In her haste she doesn't notice your multikon.

"Twelve kad-years ago," says Valeeta, "I heard the legend of the Glorid city. I became a Spy so I could search the galaxy for it. Finally, I found it—here on Delbor!"

Turn to page 44.

You rotate the keys, but you are too late! The six kad-hours are up!
Spy Center is not going to be happy about this—if they ever find out!

You and Callisto are ready to leave Delbor. You bid farewell to the Ro-zins and the king of the Choons. Now the Ro-zins also understand what you and Callisto have done for their world. And they wish to join the Choons in making Delbor a peaceful and beautiful planet.

Callisto gives them the keys and says, "I think the Glorids' dream for Delbor is going to come true!"

The Ro-zins help you carry Valeeta and Qubex on board your ship.

Turn to page 120.

Well done, Spy! The ship shrinks again.
You get it and put it in your pocket.

You hurry back to the car and drive at top speed
to the Glorid city. There are less than two kad-
hours before Delbor blows up!

Turn to page 90.

When you reach the Glorid city, you see Callisto, the king of the Choons, and the Ro-zins standing near the city entrance. Callisto wasn't able to get in!

You must get the keys to enter. Quickly you enlarge the ship. Callisto says, "Changing size has caused Valeeta and Qubex to become unconscious. Let's get the keys!"

Go on to the next page.

You and Callisto carry Valeeta and Qubex out of the ship. You take the keys from Valeeta and run to open the city entrance.

Callisto and the Ro-zins begin to tie up Valeeta and Qubex.

Turn to page 107.

The entrance opens. You take the keys and enter the city. At a distance two wild drongos are watching you. They don't look intelligent, but you'd better be careful. There may be dangerous creatures other than Valeeta here.

Turn to page 22.

You see the Glorid science building. Valeeta may be inside. You must enter secretly. High up, there is an open window.

You can swing through the window on one of the vines hanging from the trees.

Careful! If you swing on the wrong vine, you'll crash into the side of the building!

Turn to page 108.

At top speed you follow the track left by Valeeta's skimcraft.

A sudden sandstorm rushes across the desert. For a moment, you are blinded. All traces of Valeeta's skimcraft are gone!

The voice of the Poddian queen sounds in your mind. "Keep driving east. I see in Valeeta's mind that she hid her ship in the foothills in that direction when she first came to Delbor. I will tell my soldiers in the caves near there to help you."

Turn to page 116.

Valeeta runs past you into the city. She spreads her wings and flies off! She disappears behind a tall building.

Callisto has recovered. He comes up to you and says, "Spy Center warned me about Valeeta's eye beams. She can shoot only once from each eye. And she can fly for only short distances."

Callisto runs toward the power car. He says, "Hurry. We must get to the science building."

Turn to page 96.

You and Callisto race through the city. There are only a few minutes left until the generator explodes!

You arrive at the science building just as Valeeta disappears inside. The door slams shut.

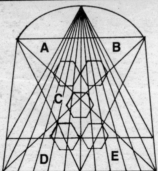

You can open the door by pushing on three of the six-sided panels. The three panels must have the same number of tension lines running through them.

Do you push panels A, B, and C?
Turn to page 99.

Do you push panels C, D, and E?
Turn to page 106.

You find the skimcraft. The craft will start if you activate the squares showing shapes that can be put together to make the body shape of a Glorid.

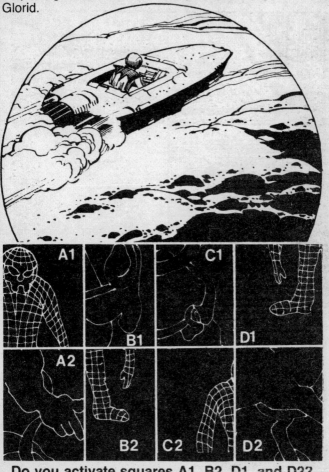

Do you activate squares A1, B2, D1, and D2?
Turn to page 114.
Do you activate squares A1, B2, C2, and D1?
Turn to page 68.
(If you can't remember what the Glorids look like, check page 33.)

You take the keys. You and Callisto examine the keys and the receptacles on the generator. You must hurry, but you must be careful!

Callisto says, "Spy, you have used these keys before, and you saw Valeeta use them on this generator. Now we must depend on you again."

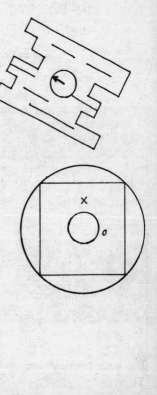

Turn to page 51.

You and Callisto are inside the science building. You run to the generator chamber.
Valeeta's ogar attacks!

"Watch out!" shouts Callisto. He knocks the
ogar into the generator pit.

Turn to page 113.

You reach the joujan and go up to it. It is friendly!

You mount it and ride away.

Turn to page 93.

The screen on the locator panel shows your co-ordinates and Valeeta's. You notice that she is approaching your landing area in the desert.

You go after her. A herd of desert buffalo scatters as you streak past.

Turn to page 102.

You see clouds of dust in the air as you approach the landing area. Valeeta passed by here. She must have attacked! Callisto, the king of the Choons, and the Ro-zins are all lying on the ground.

You race toward Callisto!

Turn to page 54.

You sent the wrong signal! The pattern is not complete.

Valeeta's ogar sees you struggling.
It might attack you.

You'd better work fast!

Go back to page 64 and try again.

You crush a leaf in your fingers and let the juice drip into Callisto's mouth. His eyes open, but he is still weak and dizzy. He looks at the plants and says, "You have given me the wrong medicine! Use the other plant!"

As fast as you can, you feed Callisto the juice of the other plant's leaves. You can see his strength beginning to return. He says, "Spy, I am too weak to help you against Valeeta. You must go after her alone."

Turn to page 78.

You hear the Poddian's thoughts. "I read Valeeta's mind. Now that her ship is destroyed, she intends to get yours. Qubex knows where it is and how to enlarge it. Hurry!" The Poddian's thoughts are fading.

You carry the Poddian into the cave. Other Poddians carry him away.

You run back to your power car and speed across the desert to the landing area. Valeeta and Qubex have enlarged the ship!

Turn to page 118.

106 You can't open the door. Then you remember the vines. You and Callisto climb the tree and swing through the open window.

Turn to page 99.

You use the keys to open the city entrance. Suddenly you hear shouts behind you. Valeeta has awakened!

She has knocked aside the Ro-zins who were guarding her. A beam of red light shoots from one of her eyes! It hits Callisto!

She runs toward you. She shoots another eye beam. You are stunned!

Turn to page 95.

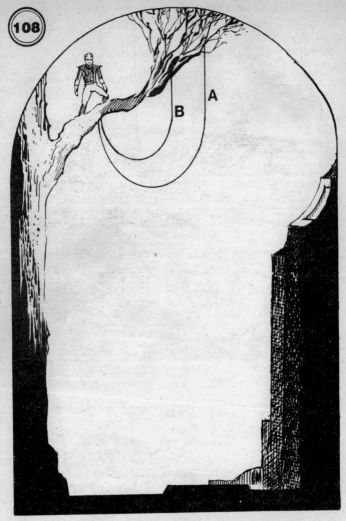

**Will you swing on vine A?
Turn to page 46.**

**Will you swing on vine B?
Turn to page 74.**

You turn bar A, and the port opens. You guide the skimcraft out into the desert. But there is no sign of Valeeta. You must find her! Only five kad-hours are left until the generator explodes.

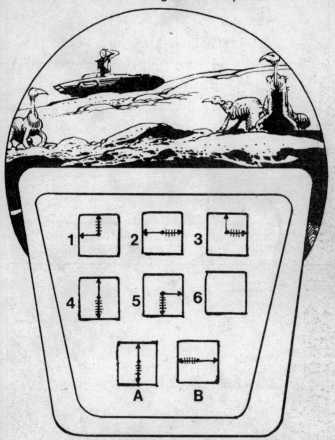

You can use the locator panel on your skimcraft to locate any other skimcraft. Press the button showing the arrow position that should appear in box 6 to complete the sequence.

Button A? Turn to page 55.
Button B? Turn to page 101.

You and Callisto hurl your multikons into the air over Valeeta's head. They collide and explode! The rebel Spy screams. She has been blinded!

Before she can recover, you wrap her in the net. But now you must disarm the generator!

Turn to page 98.

Too bad, Spy! All you can do now
is wait for . . .

The End

You can use your multikon to send a signal that will activiate the size-control mechanism on the ship.

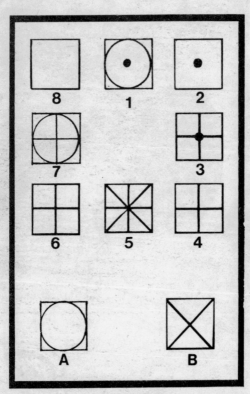

Press the shape that should appear in box Ɛ to complete the pattern on the screen.

A? Turn to page 89.

B? Turn to page 111.

Valeeta is crouched in front of the receptacles on the generator. "You'll never get past me, Spies!" she says. "We'll die together!"

Callisto leans over and whispers a plan into your ear. You and Callisto come at Valeeta from opposite sides.

Turn to page 110.

114 Too bad, Spy! You activated the wrong squares. The skimcraft automatically imprisons you.

Callisto is not dead, but his breathing is weak.
You must revive him.

You can make a medicine from the desert plant whose
leaves all have an even number of points.

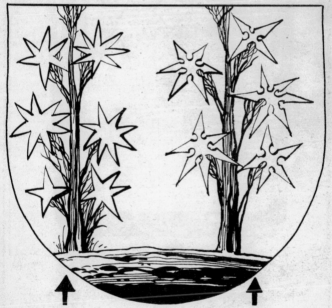

**This plant?
Turn to page 66.**

**This plant?
Turn to page 104.**

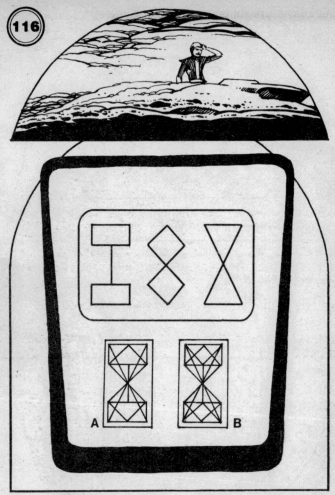

You must drive east—but the sandstorm caused you to lose your sense of direction!

Your multikon can function as a compass. You must press the shape that is made up of the three shapes on the screen.

A? Turn to page 83.

B? Turn to page 56.

Valeeta sees you coming. She shoves you against one of the Poddians.

Valeeta and Qubex jump into their skimcraft and speed away.

Turn to page 105.

Valeeta and Qubex are going on board.

If you can shrink the ship, the engines will not function and all doors will lock. Valeeta and Qubex will also be shrunk and will be trapped inside the ship!

Turn to page 112.

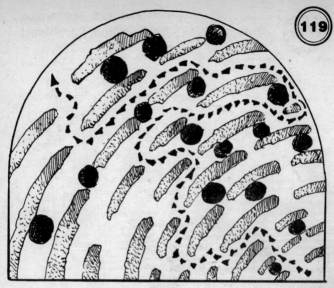

You missed the path, Spy!
It's an awfully long walk.

Turn to page 93.

Back in space, you send a message to Spy Center. You tell them that you are bringing in Valeeta and Qubex.

Callisto shakes your hand. He says, "This mission could not have succeeded without you. You are a true level 2 Spy. Congratulations!"

The End

Make sure you have all these great Interplanetary Spy books!